Big Dog
and
Little Dog

Tales of Adventure

DAV PILKEY

Big Dog and Little Dog

Tales of Adventure

Houghton Mifflin Harcourt
Boston New York

Contents

Ages	Grades	Guided Reading Level	Reading Recovery Level	Lexile® Leve
4–6	K	D	5–6	240L

Big Dog and Little Dog

To Eamon Hoyt Johnston

Big Dog and Little Dog are hungry.

Big Dog and Little Dog want food.

Here is some food for Big Dog.

Big Dog is happy.

Here is some food for Little Dog.

Little Dog is happy, too.

Big Dog and Little Dog are full.

Big Dog and Little Dog are sleepy.

Big Dog gets in the big bed.

Little Dog gets in the little bed.

Big Dog is lonely.

Little Dog is lonely, too.

Shhh.

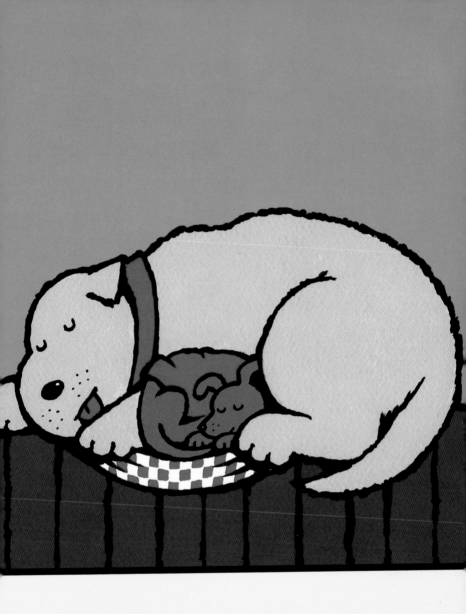

Big Dog and Little Dog are sleeping.

❧ Picture It ❧

Read the sentences below.
Which picture matches each sentence?

 Big Dog and Little Dog are sleeping.

 Here is some food for Little Dog.

 Little Dog is sleepy.

 Little Dog is lonely in his little bed.

 Hot Dog!

Can you believe these dog facts?

🐾 The Beatles song "A Day in the Life" includes a high-pitched whistle that only dogs can hear.

🐾 In ancient China, an emperor often kept a small Pekingese dog hidden up his sleeve for protection.

🐾 When Lord Byron was told his dog could not come with him to Cambridge Trinity College, he brought a bear instead.

🐾 Dogs sweat from their paws—on really hot days they leave wet footprints!

🐾 In 2003, Dr. Roger Mugford invented the "wagometer," a device that explains a dog's exact mood by measuring the wag of its tail.

Story Sequencing

The story of Big Dog and Little Dog got scrambled
Can you put the scenes in the right order?

A

B

Correct order: E, D, B, A, C

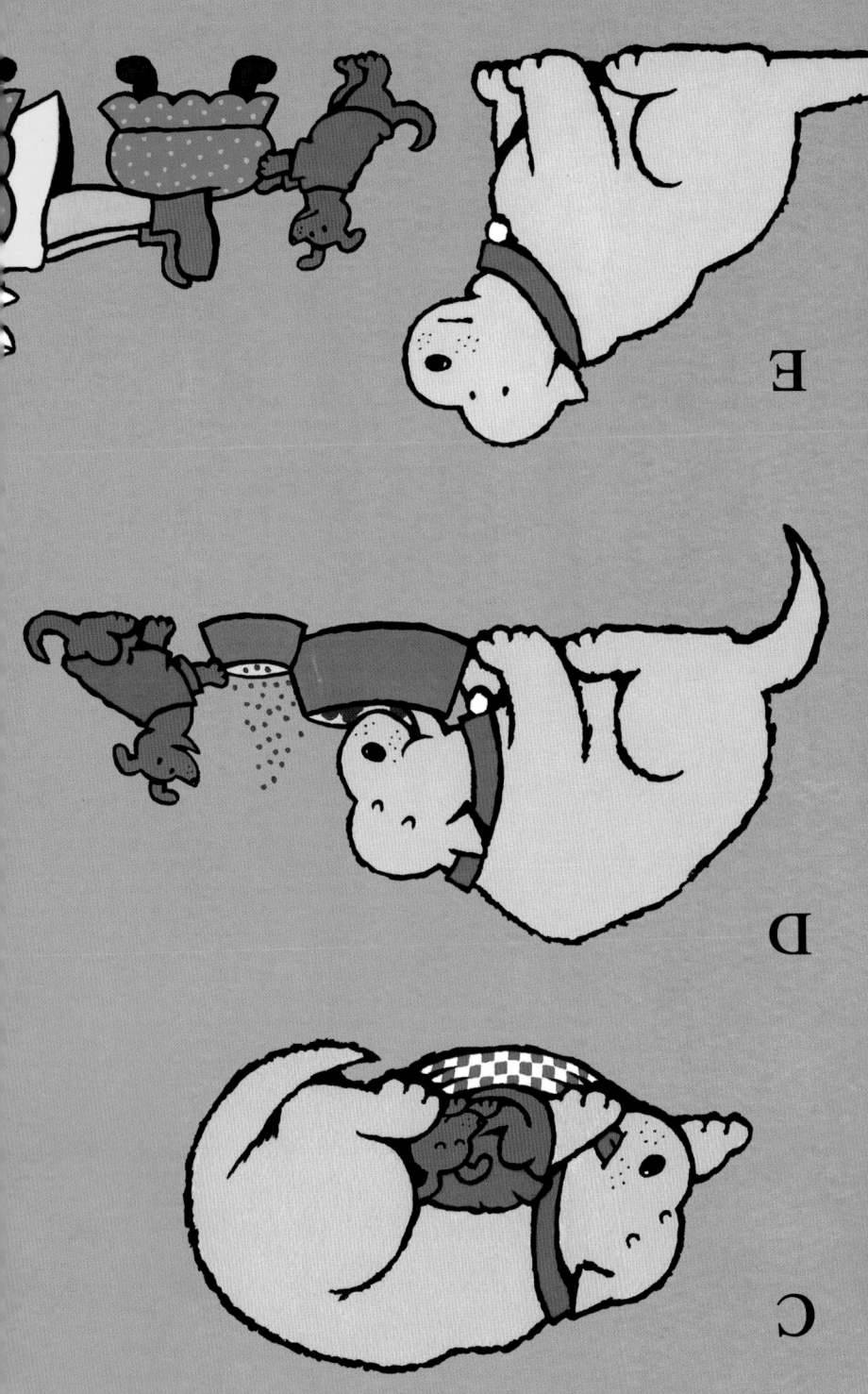

 **Dog-Libs**

Learning Nouns and Verbs

Ask a friend to make a list of seven nouns and five verbs. One verb should end in "ed" and one verb should end in "s." Use the words to complete the story. Does your friend know how to take care of a dog?

Noun - a person, place, or thing
Verb - an action

Caring for a dog is fun, but it's a lot of (noun) ! You must (verb) and (verb) and (verb) a dog. They should be fed healthy (noun) — no (noun) , (noun) , or (noun) . After dinner, they need to be (verb, ending in "ed") . If they get dirty they need a (noun) . This may seem like a lot of (noun) , but it's worth it when your dog (verb, ending in "s") your face.

Ages	Grades	Guided Reading Level	Reading Recovery Level	Lexile® Level
4–6	K	D	5–6	160L

Big Dog and Little Dog
Making a Mistake

For Samantha Jeanne Wills

Big Dog is going for a walk.

Little Dog is going, too.

Big Dog and Little Dog

see something.

What do they see?

Big Dog thinks it is a kitty.

Little Dog thinks so, too.

Sssssssssss.

But it does not *smell* like a kitty.

Big Dog smells bad.

Little Dog smells bad, too.

Big Dog and Little Dog

had a bad day.

They are going home now . . .

. . . just in time for a party!

Story Sequencing

The story of Big Dog and Little Dog's mistake got scrambled! Can you put the scenes in the right orde

A

C

B

D

E

Is that a kitty? Use your finger to trace
the best path through the maze for
Big Dog and Little Dog to reach it.

❧ Word Scramble ❧

These words from the story got mixed up! Can you unscramble them and point to the correct words in the word box? Try writing a new story with these words.

Word Box

ESE	PARTY
TYPRA	SMELL
MEHO	BAD
DAB	WALK
LELMS	KITTY
KALW	HOME
TYKIT	SEE

Bow-Wow!

Check out these amazing dog facts.

A German shepherd named Orient guided the first blind man to hike the entire Appalachian Trail— 2,100 miles!

Norwegian lundehunds have six toes on each paw so they can climb steep cliffs and their ears fold down and seal shut to keep out dirt.

Dogs and people have many of the same organs, but dogs do not have appendixes.

Almost all dogs have pink tongues except for the chow chow and the shar-pei. Their tongues are black!

Dalmatian puppies' fur is completely white when they are born and their spots appear later.

❀ Fill-in-the-Blank ❀

Use the pictures to choose the
missing word from the word box!

Word Box

smell
home
kitty
bad
walk
party

Big Dog and Little Dog are goir

for a _____.

Big Dog and Little Dog think they see a _____.

The kitty does not _____ like a kitty.

Big Dog and Little Dog smell .

Big Dog and Little Dog go .

They are just in time for the !

Ages	Grades	Guided Reading Level	Reading Recovery Level	Lexile® Lev
4–6	K	D	5–6	350L

Big Dog and Little Dog
Going for a Walk

To Nathan Douglas Libertowski

Big Dog is going for a walk.

Little Dog is going, too.

Little Dog likes to play in the mud.

Big Dog likes to eat the mud.

Little Dog likes to splash
in the puddles.

Big Dog likes to drink the puddles.

Big Dog and Little Dog

had a fun walk.

They are very dirty.

It is time to take a bath.

Big Dog and Little Dog
are in the tub.

Now it is time to dry off.

Big Dog and Little Dog

shake and shake.

Big Dog and Little Dog
are clean and dry.

Now they want to go for
another walk.

 Cause and Effect

What goes up must come down—every cause has an effect! Here is one from the story.

Cause: Big Dog and Little Dog play in mud.

Effect: Big Dog and Little Dog get dirty.

Can you think of any other causes and effects from the story?

❧ Picture It ❧

Read the sentences below.
Can you match them with the correct images?

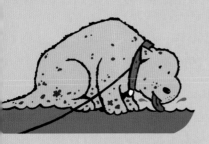

Big Dog and Little Dog are in the tub.

Little Dog likes to play in the mud.

Big Dog likes to drink the puddles.

Big Dog and Little Dog are going for a walk.

Story Sequencing

The story of Big Dog and Little Dog going for a wal got scrambled! Can you put the scenes in the right ord

A

B

C

D

E

orrect order: D, B, C, A, E

- A greyhound can run as fast as forty-five miles an hour.

- The beagle and collie are the noisiest dogs. The Akbash dog and the basenji are the quietest.

- President Lyndon Johnson had two beagles named Him and Her.

- The United States has more dogs than any other country in the world.

- The expression "the dog days of summer" goes back to ancient Roman times, when people thought Sirius, the dog star, created heat on Earth.

- Dog nose prints are as unique as human fingerprints—no two dog noses are alike.

🐾 Drawing Dogs 🐾

Big Dog and Little Dog love to go for walks.
What other adventures do you think they go on?

On a separate sheet of paper, draw your own pictures of

Big Dog and Little Dog doing things and going places!

Here are some ideas to get you started:

Big Dog and Little Dog learn a new trick.

Big Dog and Little Dog play fetch.

Big Dog and Little Dog ride in a car.

Big Dog and Little Dog howl at the moon.

Q: What do you say when your dog does
something great?

A: Pawsome!

Q: What do dogs have that no other animal has?

A: Puppies.

Q: What kind of dog can use the phone?

A: A dial-mation.

Q: Why is a tree like a big dog?

A: They both have a lot of bark.

Q: Which animal keeps the best time?

A: A watch dog.

Big Dog and Little Dog

Getting in Trouble

To Kevin Alan Libertowski

Big Dog wants to play.

Little Dog wants to play, too.

But there is nothing to play with.

What will they play with?

Big Dog and Little Dog are playing.

They are playing with the couch.

Big Dog and Little Dog
are having fun.

Big Dog and Little Dog
are being bad.

Big Dog is making a mess.

Little Dog is making a mess.

Uh-oh.

Big Dog is in trouble.

Little Dog is in trouble, too.

Big Dog and Little Dog are sorry.

They will be good from now on.

❖ Spot the Differences ❖

There are eight differences between the
top picture and the bottom picture.
Can you find them all?

🐾 Word Scramble 🐾

These words from the story got mixed up! Can you scramble them and point to the correct words in the rd box? Try writing a new story with these words!

Word Box

AYPL	FUN
UCOCH	LITTLE
NFU	PLAY
DAB	COUCH
IGB	GOOD
LETLIT	BAD
DOGO	BIG

Dog-Libs

Learning Nouns and Verbs

Ask a friend to make a list of
six nouns and three verbs.
Use the words to complete the story.
How silly is your new story?

Noun - a person, place, or thing
Verb - an action

Dogs are very playful. They will (verb) with a (noun) , a (noun) , or a (noun) . Sometimes, dogs will be very bad and play with a (noun) . When they do that, they make a big (noun) . When dogs (verb) , they should not (verb) with a (noun) !

Fill-in-the-Blank

Choose the missing word from the
word box to complete these sentences!

Word Box

fun
mess
play
trouble
couch
bad

Big Dog wants to _____.

Big Dog and Little Dog are playing with the _____.

Big Dog and Little Dog are having _____.

Big Dog and Little Dog are being _____.

Big Dog and Little Dog are making a _____.

Big Dog is in big _____.

Ages	Grades	Guided Reading Level	Reading Recovery Level	Lexile® Level
4–6	K	D	5–6	240L

Big Dog and Little Dog
Wearing Sweaters

To Robert Martin Staenberg

Little Dog has a sweater.

Big Dog does not have a sweater.

Big Dog is sad.

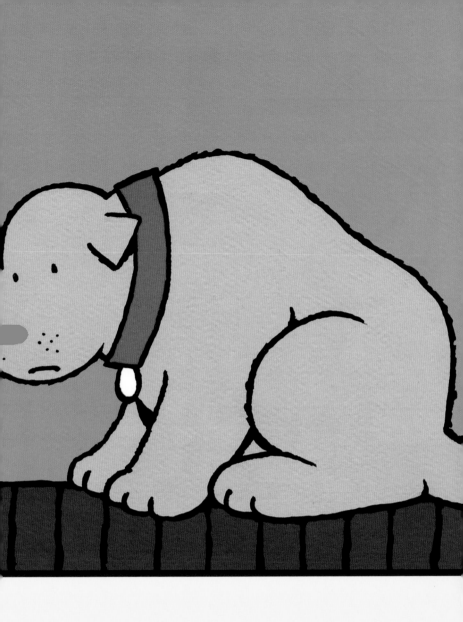

Big Dog wants a sweater, too.

Big Dog is looking for a sweater.

Little Dog is helping.

Big Dog has found a sweater.

Hooray for Big Dog!

Big Dog is putting the sweater on.

Little Dog is helping some more.

Now Little Dog has a sweater.

And Big Dog has a sweater.

Big Dog and Little Dog
are warm and happy.

Good night.

🐾 Lost in the Maze 🐾

Can you help Little Dog find a sweater for Big Dog? Use your finger to trace the path!

Word Search

Find the hidden words from the story!
Remember, words may go across, down, or diagonally!

Word Box

SWEATER	DOG
HELP	HOORAY
WARM	HAPPY
BIG	LITTLE

```
Y Q D W A R M R
S W I B I G E G
O D L I T T L E
N O H L A Y L D
C G O E P O J I
X L W P L I A Y
O S A A D P Y N
G H O O R A Y B
```

🐾 Story Sequencing 🐾

The story of Big Dog's sweater got scrambled!
Can you put the scenes in the right order?

C

D

E

Correct order: D, B, E, A, C

Big Dog does not have a sweater.

Big Dog has found a sweater.

Little Dog helps Big Dog put on the sweater.

Big Dog and Little Dog are warm and happy.